The Ebony Frame

*A Gothic Love Story of Art, Obsession,
and the Occult*

A Modern Translation

Adapted for the Contemporary Reader

Edith Nesbit

Translated by Tim Zengerink

Table of Contents

Preface - Message to the Reader

What If You Could Help Rebuild the Greatest Library in Human History?

Thousands of years ago, the Library of Alexandria stood as the crown jewel of human achievement — a sanctuary where the collected wisdom of every known civilization was gathered, preserved, and shared freely.

And then, it was lost.

Through fire, conquest, and the slow erosion of time, humanity lost not just books — but ideas, dreams, discoveries, and stories that could have changed the world forever.

Today, the Library of Alexandria lives again — and you are invited to be a part of its restoration.

Our mission is simple yet profound:

To rebuild the greatest library the world has ever known, and to translate all timeless works into every language and dialect, so that no seeker of knowledge is ever left behind again.

By joining our movement to rebuild the modern Library of Alexandria, you become part of an unprecedented mission:

- **Unlimited Access to the Greatest Audiobooks & eBooks Ever Written:**

  Instantly explore thousands of legendary works—Plato, Shakespeare, Jane Austen, Leo Tolstoy, and countless more. All instantly available to read or listen, placing a complete literary universe at your fingertips.

- **Beautiful Paperback & Deluxe Editions at Printing Cost**

  Own any title as an elegant paperback, deluxe hardcover, or stunning collectible boxset—offered to you at true printing cost, delivered straight to your door. Build your personal Library of Alexandria, crafted for beauty, built for durability, and worthy of proud display.

- **Fresh Translations for Modern Readers—in Every Language & Dialect**

  Enjoy timeless masterpieces reimagined in clear, contemporary language—no more outdated phrases or obscure references. Alongside the original versions, we're tirelessly translating these classics into every language and dialect imaginable, ensuring accessibility and understanding across cultures and generations.

- **Join a Global Renaissance of Literature & Knowledge**

  You directly support expanding our library, publishing deluxe editions at true cost, translating works into all global languages, and bringing humanity's greatest stories to people everywhere. By joining today, you're not just preserving a legacy of masterpieces; you set in motion a powerful wave of literary accessibility.

Become a Torchbearer of Knowledge.

Join us for free now at **LibraryofAlexandria.com**

Together, we will ensure that the light of human wisdom never fades again.

With gratitude and a shared love of knowledge,

The Modern Library of Alexandria Team

Visit:

www.libraryofalexandria.com

Or scan the code below:

Introduction

Obsession, Art, and the Eternal Return of Desire

Edith Nesbit, widely celebrated for her pioneering contributions to children's literature, is less commonly remembered for her chilling, adult-oriented ghost stories. Yet works such as Man-Size in Marble, John Charrington's Wedding, and most hauntingly, The Ebony Frame, reveal her mastery of psychological horror and supernatural tension. First published in 1893, The Ebony Frame is a remarkable example of fin de siècle gothic fiction: moody, seductive, rich with moral ambiguity, and propelled by an intense emotional undercurrent. Beneath its supernatural premise lies a tale of guilt, temptation, eternal longing, and the price of breaking sacred bonds—whether of love, fidelity, or the soul itself.

In its compact structure, The Ebony Frame distills the gothic to its most potent elements. The story follows a man named Lawrence, a seemingly rational and worldly gentleman who inherits a house from a distant aunt. While exploring the property, he discovers a beautiful woman's portrait encased in an ebony frame—an artwork so enchanting that he is instantly overwhelmed with passion for the painted figure. This romantic obsession soon transcends fantasy, as the woman in the painting begins to speak to him, claiming to be his true love from a past life. Driven by this spectral seduction, Lawrence turns away from his real-life fiancée, only to plunge into a terrifying web of possession, fate, and irreversible choices.

Nesbit plays masterfully with the tropes of haunted art, past-life romance, and the doppelgänger mythos, drawing readers into a narrative where every glance, every word, and every emotional choice holds existential weight. The story is not merely about ghosts, but about the nature of memory, desire, and moral collapse. It explores how love can become a trap, how beauty can ensnare the will, and how the past, once unearthed, can take a life of its own.

In this introduction, we will explore The Ebony Frame through three major thematic lenses: its treatment of obsession and the idea of the "eternal lover"; its gothic use of art and architecture to signify emotional and metaphysical distortion; and its moral vision of sin, consequence, and the boundaries between love and damnation. We will also consider its unique place in Edith Nesbit's broader literary career, as well as its contribution to the evolution of supernatural fiction during the transition from Victorian to Edwardian sensibilities. As we shall see, this "little" ghost story casts a long shadow—one that continues to enthrall, disturb, and provoke long after the final page.

The Haunted Lover:
Past Lives, False Memory, and Fatal Desire

One of the most arresting elements in The Ebony Frame is its central concept: that love can transcend death and return across time, reasserting itself with hypnotic force. The woman in the painting, believed to be a former lover from a previous incarnation, appears not only as a ghost but as an emotional force that overwhelms Lawrence's sense of self. She is not remembered—she remembers him, and calls him back into the drama they once shared.

This inversion of the typical ghost story structure— where the haunting is not about revenge or unfinished business but about rekindled passion—is part of what makes the tale so unsettling. The idea that one could be so utterly possessed by the past, so deeply intertwined with a lover from another life, that it would cause one to betray all present commitments, creates a compelling psychological tension. Is this true love rediscovered? Or is it a supernatural deception? Nesbit leaves room for both interpretations, adding to the tale's eerie ambiguity.

The frame—black, polished, and commanding—functions not only as a literal container for the portrait but also as a symbol of fate. It is the threshold through which the past breaches the present. It encases not just the image of the woman, but the emotional contract that Lawrence unwittingly reactivates. His act of staring at the painting is not passive—it is an invocation. And once invoked, the past demands payment.

Lawrence's descent is rapid and irreversible. Within days, he abandons his living fiancée, repudiates his responsibilities, and devotes himself entirely to a ghost. He does not question the morality or reality of this shift; he is consumed. This narrative arc offers a powerful allegory for addiction, narcissism, or any overpowering obsession that obliterates reason. It is not merely supernatural horror—it is emotional annihilation. The idea that love can be so strong as to override not only present reality but the integrity of the soul is a gothic theme that Nesbit executes with tragic clarity.

The woman in the painting is not portrayed as overtly malevolent—she is alluring, wounded, devoted—but her love is possessive. Eternal. Unforgiving. Whether she is real or hallucinated, angel or demon, is less important than the fact that Lawrence chooses her over life. And that choice costs him everything.

The Architecture of Entrapment: The House, the Frame, and the Illusion of Control

The setting of The Ebony Frame plays a crucial role in amplifying the story's dread. Like many classic gothic tales, it begins in a house inherited under ambiguous circumstances—a place saturated with personal and ancestral memory. This space, left untouched for years, becomes a psychic echo chamber, ready to resurrect the desires and sins of those who once lived there.

As Lawrence explores the house, it becomes clear that it is not just a location—it is an active participant in the story. The air is heavy. The silence feels expectant. The room with the painting becomes a portal of sorts, a site of transformation. Nesbit uses the architecture to express Lawrence's mental state: the deeper he ventures into the house, the deeper he falls into obsession. The more time he spends with the portrait, the more unmoored he becomes from reality.

The ebony frame itself is both elegant and oppressive. Its rich, dark surface suggests value and status, but also morbidity. The frame is what gives the portrait its weight and power. It delineates the boundary between this world and the other—and like all gothic thresholds, it is both barrier and invitation. When the woman steps out of the painting (or seems to), the frame becomes the broken seal, the breach that lets the past in.

What's particularly powerful in Nesbit's rendering is the seamless transition between reality and dream, between hallucination and experience. Lawrence's psychological state deteriorates not because he is confronted with horror, but because horror feels like love. The disorientation that follows is both emotional and spatial. He no longer knows what is real, and neither do we.

This gothic destabilization—of time, space, memory, and emotion—is central to the story's haunting effect. The house is no longer a home. The painting is no longer art. The past is no longer dead. Every surface, every object, every memory becomes suspect. And when Lawrence finally realizes what he has done, the horror is not that the ghost was real—but that he chose it willingly.

The Weight of Consequence: Love, Betrayal, and Moral Reckoning

Unlike many ghost stories of its era, The Ebony Frame is not merely a tale of revenge or spiritual imbalance. It is a meditation on personal responsibility, on the choices we make and the lies we tell ourselves to justify them. Lawrence is not cursed by the painting—he is tempted by it. His ruin is not the result of supernatural malevolence, but of his own emotional weakness and moral cowardice.

In this way, Nesbit aligns herself with the deeper tradition of the moral gothic, in which the supernatural functions not as random terror but as mirror. The ghost in The Ebony Frame reflects Lawrence's own unacknowledged desires—his longing for passion, his dissatisfaction with convention, and his willingness to abandon virtue for beauty. What he receives is not punishment but truth. The ghost does not destroy him. He destroys himself.

This moral ambiguity gives the story its staying power. We pity Lawrence, but we also recognize his failure. We are drawn to the passion he finds, but we recoil from the cost. Nesbit doesn't offer a simple moral lesson. She offers a gothic crucible—a place where the soul is tested, where illusion and reality blur, and where every choice echoes eternally.

In its final moments, the story turns from romantic obsession to existential horror. Lawrence is not merely heartbroken—he is damned. His soul has been bartered. The woman he loved is not saved, and neither is he. The frame is empty. The house is silent. The world moves on. But Lawrence is no longer part of it.

This chilling conclusion cements The Ebony Frame as one of the most psychologically resonant ghost stories of the Victorian period. It speaks to eternal themes—desire, betrayal, memory, fate—and distills them into a tale as compact as it is devastating.

With this story, Edith Nesbit stepped beyond her reputation as a children's writer and proved herself a master of adult gothic horror. The Ebony Frame is not merely a tale of ghosts—it is a tale of what haunts us when we let go of who we are, and embrace what we most desperately want.

Even when that want is the thing that will consume us.

The Ebony Frame

To be rich feels amazing—especially after you've been broke for so long. I'd spent years as a struggling writer in Fleet Street, picking up small reporting jobs and writing pieces that no one seemed to care about. It was hard work and didn't suit my background—after all, I was descended from the Dukes of Picardy.

When my Aunt Dorcas died and left me a house in Chelsea and seven hundred pounds a year, it felt like I had everything I could ever want. Even Mildred Mayhew, who had once seemed like the love of my life, started to matter a little less. We weren't engaged, but I rented a room in her mother's house, sang duets with her, and gave her gifts when I could afford it—not often. She was kind and sweet, and I had always planned to marry her someday. It's comforting to know someone is thinking about you, supporting you quietly in the background, and would say "yes" if you ever asked, "Will you marry me?"

But after my aunt's death, and especially since Mildred was out of town visiting friends, my thoughts started drifting away from her.

Not long after the funeral, I was sitting in my aunt's armchair in front of the fire, in the drawing room of my own house. My own house! It felt grand—but also a little lonely. I did think of Mildred for a moment.

The room was nicely decorated with rosewood furniture and damask fabrics. A few decent oil paintings hung on the walls, but above the fireplace was a terribly ugly print called The Trial of Lord William Russell, framed in a heavy, dark frame. I stood up to get a better look. I'd visited my aunt many times, but I didn't remember ever seeing that frame before. It looked too fancy for a print—like it was made for a real painting. The wood was beautiful ebony, carved in a detailed and delicate design. I found myself getting more curious about it.

When Jane, my aunt's longtime housemaid—who I had kept on with the rest of the small staff—brought in the lamp, I asked her how long that print had been hanging there.

"Missus only bought the picture two days before she got sick," Jane said. "But the frame—she didn't want to buy a new one, so she got that out of the attic. There's loads of strange old stuff up there, sir."

"Has the frame been here long?" I asked.

"Oh yes, sir. Long before my time. I've been here nearly seven years. There was a picture in it once, too. It's still upstairs—but it's so dark and ugly it might as well be a lump of coal."

That made me want to see it. What if my aunt had owned some old masterpiece she couldn't appreciate?

Right after breakfast the next morning, I went up to the attic.

It was packed with furniture that looked like it belonged in a curiosity shop. The rest of the house was decorated in solid mid-Victorian style, but anything that didn't match had ended up up here. There were papier-mâché tables with pearl inlays, stiff chairs with twisted legs and faded cushions, carved fire screens with beaded banners, old oak desks with brass handles, and a tiny work table with torn silk drooping from it. The sunlight blazed in as I opened the blinds, lighting up the dust. I made a mental note to fix up these lovely old things and bring them downstairs, and send the Victorian furniture up here instead.

But first, I had a mission: find the ugly painting that looked "black as the chimney back."

Soon enough, buried behind a pile of fenders and boxes, I found it.

Jane confirmed it was the right one. I carefully carried it downstairs and examined it. You couldn't tell what it was supposed to be. The colors were faded into a dark blur. There was one darker patch in the middle, but I couldn't tell if it was a person, a tree, or a house. The painting was on a thick wooden panel, with leather wrapped around the edges.

I thought about sending it to a professional restorer—but then decided to try cleaning a small corner myself. Using soap, a sponge, and a nailbrush, I scrubbed hard. But no image appeared—just plain oak wood. I tried the other side, with Jane watching curiously. Same result. Then it hit me—why was the panel so thick?

I tore off the leather binding. The panel split and fell apart in a cloud of dust.

It had been two separate paintings, nailed together, face to face.

I propped them both against the wall—and then staggered back in shock.

One of them was a perfect portrait of me. Every detail, every expression—exactly me. But I was wearing clothes from the time of King James the First. How was this even possible? When had this painting been made? And how could it have happened without me knowing?

Was this some odd trick or secret plan of my aunt's?

"Wow, sir!" Jane squealed beside me. "What a lovely photo! Was it from a costume party or something?"

"Yes," I muttered. "I... I don't think I need anything else right now. You can go."

She left, and I turned back to the second painting. It was of a woman—stunningly beautiful. I couldn't stop staring at her. She had a straight nose, gently arched brows, full lips, delicate hands, and large, glowing eyes that seemed to shine. She wore a black velvet dress and was shown from the waist up. Her arms rested on a table, and her head leaned on her hands, but her face looked straight ahead. Her eyes seemed to lock with mine in a way that was both powerful and hard to describe.

On the table next to her were compasses, shiny tools I didn't recognize, books, a goblet, papers, and pens. I noticed those things later. At first, I just stood there, staring into her eyes, completely mesmerized. I had never seen eyes like hers. They had the softness of a child's or a dog's gaze but the power of a queen's.

"Should I sweep up the dust, sir?" Jane had returned, probably too curious to stay away. I nodded and quickly turned my portrait away from her. I didn't want her to see the woman in the black dress.

When I was alone again, I took down The Trial of Lord William Russell and placed the woman's portrait in the heavy ebony frame.

Then I ordered a new frame for my own portrait. After all, the two had been together for so long—I couldn't bring myself to separate them. Maybe that sounds sentimental, but I couldn't help it.

When the new frame arrived, I hung my picture on the wall opposite the fireplace. I went through all of my aunt's old papers, hoping to find something—anything—about these two portraits. But I found nothing. I only learned that all the old furniture, along with the pictures, had come to my aunt from my great-uncle after his death. I might've thought the resemblance in my portrait was just a family one… except everyone who visited immediately pointed out how striking the likeness was. I ended up going with Jane's "costume party" story whenever anyone asked.

That should have been the end of it. And it would've been—if there weren't clearly more to the story.

Back then, though, I thought it was over.

I went to visit Mildred. I invited her and her mother to come stay with me. I tried not to look too long at the painting in the ebony frame. But I couldn't forget the first time I met that woman's gaze, and how strangely it made me feel. I didn't want to feel that again.

I made some changes to the house to get it ready for Mildred's visit. I brought some of the older furniture down from the attic. After a long day of arranging and rearranging, I finally sat down in front of the fire. Relaxed and tired, I leaned back in the chair and, without thinking, looked up at her painting again.

Her deep hazel eyes locked with mine once more, and I couldn't look away. It was like I was under some kind of spell. You know that odd feeling when you stare into your own reflection for too long? It was like that— but stronger. My eyes stung, like I might cry.

"I wish," I whispered, "oh, how I wish you were real and not just a picture. Come down to me—please, come down!"

I chuckled at how silly I sounded—but even while laughing, I reached my arms toward her.

I wasn't tired. I wasn't drunk. I was completely awake and clear-headed. But as I held out my arms, I swear I saw her eyes widen. Her lips quivered. And, even if it sounds crazy, her hands moved just a little— and the faintest smile crossed her face.

I jumped up. "This is getting ridiculous," I said out loud. "Firelight can really play tricks on your eyes. I need to turn on the lamp."

I walked toward the bell to call for help. My hand was just about to ring it when I heard a noise behind me. I froze and turned around—the bell still not rung. The fire had burned low, and shadows filled the corners of the room. But behind the tall embroidered chair, there was something darker than just a shadow.

"I've got to face this," I told myself. "If I don't, I'll never be able to live with myself." I stepped away from the bell, grabbed the poker, and hit the dull coals until they lit up. Bright flames danced up. Then I turned and looked at the picture.

The ebony frame was empty.

From the shadow near the chair came a soft sound, like rustling fabric—and out of the shadows, the woman from the painting stepped forward, walking straight toward me.

I've never felt fear like that before. I couldn't move. I couldn't speak. Either the rules of the world had stopped working, or I had lost my mind. I stood there shaking, but I didn't run. I just watched as her black velvet dress brushed across the rug, closer and closer to me.

Then, I felt her touch—her hand, soft and warm, as real as mine—and I heard her voice, low and gentle: "You called me. I came."

The moment I heard her speak, the world shifted. It stopped feeling terrifying or impossible. It just felt... right. Like it was always meant to be. Like nothing else mattered.

I reached for her hand and looked back at the painting—but I couldn't see it anymore in the flickering firelight. "We know each other," I said.

"Oh yes," she whispered. "We're not strangers."

Her glowing eyes locked on mine. Her lips were close. With a cry—one full of love and relief, like finding the one thing you thought you'd lost forever— I wrapped my arms around her. She wasn't a ghost. She was real. She was mine.

"How long has it been?" I asked. "How long since I lost you?"

She leaned back slightly, her hands resting behind my head. "How could I know?" she said. "There's no time in hell."

It wasn't a dream. I swear, it wasn't. I wish it had been—dreams fade. But this was real. I saw her eyes, heard her voice, felt her lips on my skin. I held her hands in mine. That night was the greatest moment of my life.

At first, we barely spoke. Just being there together was enough. After all the years of loneliness, all the pain, she was in my arms again.

It's hard to explain how powerful it was. How real it all felt. I left her in that chair for a moment, went down to the kitchen, and told the maids I didn't need anything else. I told them I was working and didn't want to be disturbed.

I even brought up more firewood myself. When I returned, she was still there, sitting just as I left her. She turned her head when I walked in. I saw the love in her eyes. I dropped to my knees in front of her and thanked fate that I had been born—because it led me to this.

I didn't think once of Mildred. Everything before this felt like a dream. She was the only thing that had ever felt real.

"I've been wondering," she said after a while, once we had talked and smiled the way people do after being apart for a long time, "how much do you remember about our past?"

"I only remember that I love you—and that I've loved you my whole life."

"You don't remember anything else? Not even a little?"

"Only that I belong to you. That we've both been through so much. But tell me, my love, tell me everything you remember. Help me understand. Actually... maybe I don't need to understand. It's enough that we're here, together."

If it was a dream, why have I never had one like it again?

She leaned close, resting her arm around my neck and gently pulling my head to her shoulder. "I guess I'm a ghost," she said with a soft laugh. That laugh stirred up old memories I almost remembered—but not quite.

"But we both know better, don't we? I'll tell you what you've forgotten. We were in love—you haven't forgotten that—and we were supposed to get married when you came back from the war. Our portraits were painted before you left. You know I was more educated than most women back then. When you were gone, people started saying I was a witch. They put me on trial. Just because I studied the stars and knew things other women didn't, they tied me to a stake and burned me alive. And you were so far away..."

She trembled. Her whole body shook. And somehow, my touch—my kiss—was enough to calm even that terrible memory.

"The night before they burned me, the devil came to me," she said. "I was innocent before that—you know I was. And even then, I only gave in for you! Because I loved you so deeply. He offered me a deal, and I took it. I gave up my soul to eternal fire, but I got something in return. I got the right to come back, through my portrait, if anyone looked at it and wished for me. As long as it stayed in its ebony frame. That frame wasn't made by human hands. I also earned something else—but I'll tell you about that in a moment. They burned me, called me a witch. It was the worst pain you can imagine—people staring, wood crackling, smoke choking the air…"

"Don't, my love. Please, no more."

"That night, my mother sat by my picture and cried out, 'Come back, my poor, lost child!' So I came. My heart was so full of hope. But she pulled away from me. She screamed, said I was a ghost. She had our portraits covered and locked in that frame again. But she had promised mine would always stay there. Through all those years, your face was always next to mine."

She stopped for a moment.

"But the man you loved?" I asked.

"You came back home. But my portrait was gone. They lied to you, and you ended up marrying someone else. Still, I knew someday you would walk the earth again—and I'd find you."

"What was the other thing you gained?" I asked.

She answered slowly. "The other gift—the one I gave my soul for—is this: if you give up your hopes of heaven, too, I can stay here. I can stay in this world as a real woman. I can be your wife. After all these years, finally... finally!"

"If I give up my soul," I said slowly—and it didn't even seem like a crazy thing to say—"if I give that up, I get you? That doesn't make sense. You are my soul."

She looked right into my eyes. And in that moment, I felt like our souls became one.

"Then you really choose me?" she said. "You're truly choosing to give up heaven for me—just like I gave it up for you?"

"I won't give up heaven for anything," I told her. "But tell me what I can do so that you and I can build a heaven right here—starting now."

"I'll tell you tomorrow," she said. "Be here alone tomorrow night. Midnight is ghost time, isn't it? That's when I'll step out of the painting—and I won't go back. I'll live with you, grow old, die, and be buried like anyone else. But before all that, we'll live, truly live, my love."

I rested my head on her knee. A heavy sleepiness came over me. Holding her hand to my face, I drifted off. When I woke up, pale November morning light was coming through the window. My head was lying on my own arm. I sat up quickly—my head was no longer on her knee, but on the needlework cushion of the stiff-backed chair.

I jumped to my feet. I was cold, confused, and still half-dreaming, but I looked toward the picture. There she was—my love, sitting just as before. I reached out to her, but stopped myself before calling out. She had said midnight. I would respect her word. Even her smallest wish was my command.

So I stood silently, staring into her soft, grey-green eyes until tears of joy filled my own.

"Oh, my love, how will I make it through the hours until I see you again?"

There wasn't a single thought in my head that any of it had been a dream. Not for a moment.

I staggered up to my bedroom, fell across the bed, and slept deeply, without dreams. When I woke up, it was noon. Mildred and her mother were coming for lunch.

At one o'clock, I remembered Mildred... and that she even existed.

That's when it really felt like I was dreaming.

With a strange sense that nothing else mattered anymore—nothing without her—I gave the necessary orders to welcome my guests. When Mildred and her mother arrived, I greeted them politely. I said all the right things, but it didn't feel like me. My voice sounded far away. My heart wasn't in it.

Things were fine—just bearable—until we had tea in the drawing room.

Mildred and her mother chatted away, sharing shallow, polite stories. I sat through it, like someone clinging to the thought of heaven while stuck in a boring, endless afternoon. I kept glancing at my love in the ebony frame. As long as she came to me again, nothing else mattered. I could sit through anything.

But then Mildred looked at the painting and said, "She sure thinks highly of herself, doesn't she? A dramatic type? One of your old flames, Mr. Devigne?"

Her words hit me like a slap. I felt helpless and annoyed. And it only got worse when Mildred—how had I ever thought her pretty?—flopped into the tall chair. She covered the delicate needlework cushion with her frilly dress and added, "Well, silence means yes! Who is she, Mr. Devigne? Come on, tell us! I bet she has a wild backstory."

Poor Mildred, smiling so confidently, thinking she was charming me. Sitting in that chair—the same chair my love had sat in when she told me her story. I couldn't take it.

"Don't sit there," I said. "It's not comfortable."

But she just laughed and said, "Oh no! Can't I even sit where your black velvet lady sat?"

I looked at the painting. It was the same chair. And there Mildred sat—where my true love had been.

Suddenly, the idea that Mildred was real, and everything else just fantasy, hit me hard. What if this really was the truth? What if, by chance, Mildred had ended up not just in that chair—but in that place in my life?

I stood up.

"I hope I'm not being rude," I said. "But I really have to step out now."

I don't even remember what excuse I made. The lie came easily.

Mildred looked upset, but I told her and her mother not to wait for me at dinner. Then I left. In just a few minutes, I was out in the cool, cloudy autumn air— alone, and free to think about her. Only her.

I walked for hours through streets and across empty squares. Over and over again, I remembered everything—each look, every word, every time she touched my hand or kissed me. I felt completely, unbelievably happy.

Mildred was gone from my mind. My lady in the ebony frame filled my whole heart and soul.

When I heard the clock strike eleven through the fog, I turned around and went home.

But when I reached my street, I saw a crowd of people standing in front of a house, and the air was glowing red. My house was on fire.

I pushed through the crowd, heart racing. I had to save the picture—her picture.

I ran up the steps. Through the smoke and noise, it felt like a dream. I saw Mildred at the upstairs window, crying and wringing her hands.

"Come back!" a fireman shouted. "We'll get the young lady out safely."

But what about my lady?

The stairs were breaking apart, full of smoke and heat like fire from hell. I ran to the room where her portrait hung. Strangely, I didn't think of the painting as being her—just something we would want to keep through our happy life together.

As I reached the first floor, I felt arms wrap around my neck. The smoke was too thick to see clearly.

"Save me," someone whispered.

I carried her—whoever she was—down the burning stairs and into the street. As soon as I held her, I knew it was Mildred.

"Everyone's safe!" a fireman yelled.

The flames shot through every window. The sky glowed brighter and redder. I broke away from the people holding me back. I ran up the steps again. I climbed the stairs.

Suddenly it hit me: "As long as my picture stays in the ebony frame." What if the fire destroyed both?

I fought through the smoke and heat, choking and gasping. I had to reach it. I had to save it. I reached the drawing room.

And there—through the fire—I saw her. I swear I saw her. She reached out her arms to me, and I tried to run to her. I came too late.

Before I could grab her—or even cry out—the floor gave way beneath me. I fell into the flames.

They rescued me. How? I don't know. And I don't care. They pulled me out—curse them for it.

Everything was destroyed. My aunt's furniture, all of it, gone. My friends tried to comfort me, saying the furniture was insured and it wasn't a real loss.

Not a loss? They didn't know what I had lost.

That's how I found—and lost—the only love I ever had.

I swear, with all my heart, that it wasn't a dream. No dream ever felt like that. Dreams are full of longing, fear, sadness. But a dream like that—full of joy, so perfect and real?

No, the rest of my life is the dream.

So why did I marry Mildred? Why did I grow boring and dull and "successful"?

Because none of this is real. She was real. And what does it matter what you do… in a dream?

The End

Thank You for Reading

Dear Reader,

We hope this timeless classic has sparked your imagination and enriched your literary journey. Now that you've turned the final page, we want to share a vision for the future of reading—one where every classic you've ever wanted to explore is at your fingertips, in a format that best suits your life.

We'd like to invite you to gain immediate, unlimited digital & audiobook access to hundreds of the most treasured literary classics ever written—along with the option to secure deluxe paperback, hardcover & box set editions at printing cost. Together, we can spark a new global literary renaissance alongside our small, independent publishing house called "The Library of Alexandria."

Thousands of years ago, the Library of Alexandria stood as a beacon of knowledge—until it was lost to history. We aim to reignite that spirit of preservation and discovery right now, in the modern age—only this time, it's accessible to all, in every language and every format.

Picture a world where every timeless classic, novel, poem, or philosophical treatise is not only available to read but also updated for today's readers—modernized, translated into any language or dialect, and ready to enjoy in any format you choose, whether that is in an eBook, audiobook, paperback, or deluxe hardcover & box set version a printing cost.

By joining our movement to rebuild the modern Library of Alexandria, you become part of an unprecedented mission to offer:

- **Unlimited Audiobook & eBook Access to the Greatest Classics of All Time**

  Instantly explore thousands of legendary works, from Plato and Shakespeare to Jane Austen and Leo Tolstoy. All are instantly ready to read or listen to, giving you a complete literary universe at your fingertips.

- **Paperback & Deluxe Editions at Printing Costs:**

  Purchase any title in a paperback, deluxe hardbound, or deluxe boxset edition at printing costs, shipped right to your doorstep. Curate your personal library of Alexandria with editions worthy of display—crafted to last, designed to captivate, and delivered straight to your door.

- **Modern translations for Contemporary Readers in all languages and dialects**

  Discover a vast selection of classics reimagined in clear, current language—no more struggling with outdated phrases or obscure references. Next to the original versions, we aim to offer translations in as many languages and dialects as possible.

  As we continue our translation efforts and add new languages, readers everywhere can connect with these works as if they were written today. By bridging linguistic divides, you're contributing to ensuring that these timeless stories become more meaningful, accessible, and inspiring for people across the globe.

- **Your Personal Library of Alexandria:**

  Over the months and years, you'll curate a unique physical archive of classics—each volume a testament to your taste, curiosity, and love of knowledge. It's not just about owning books—it's about curating a cultural legacy you'll cherish and pass down for generations to come.

- **Join a Global Literary Renaissance:**

  Your support fuels an ongoing mission: allowing us to reinvest in offering deluxe print editions (including special boxsets) at their true cost, broaden the range of available formats and translations, and extend the reach of these works to new audiences worldwide. By joining today, you're not just preserving a legacy of masterpieces; you set in motion a powerful wave of literary accessibility.

We are more than a publisher—we're a movement, and we can't do it alone. Your support lets us scale our mission, preserving and reimagining history's greatest works for tomorrow's readers.

Become a Torchbearer of knowledge.

Thank you for picking up this book and allowing us into your literary journey. As you turn the pages, know that you're part of something larger: a global effort to keep these stories alive, share their wisdom across borders and generations, and spark a true cultural revival for the modern era.

If this resonates with you—please consider taking the next step by visiting:

www.libraryofalexandria.com

With gratitude and a shared love of knowledge,

The Modern Library of Alexandria Team

Visit:

www.libraryofalexandria.com

Or scan the code below:

* 9 7 8 1 8 0 6 2 9 1 5 4 0 *